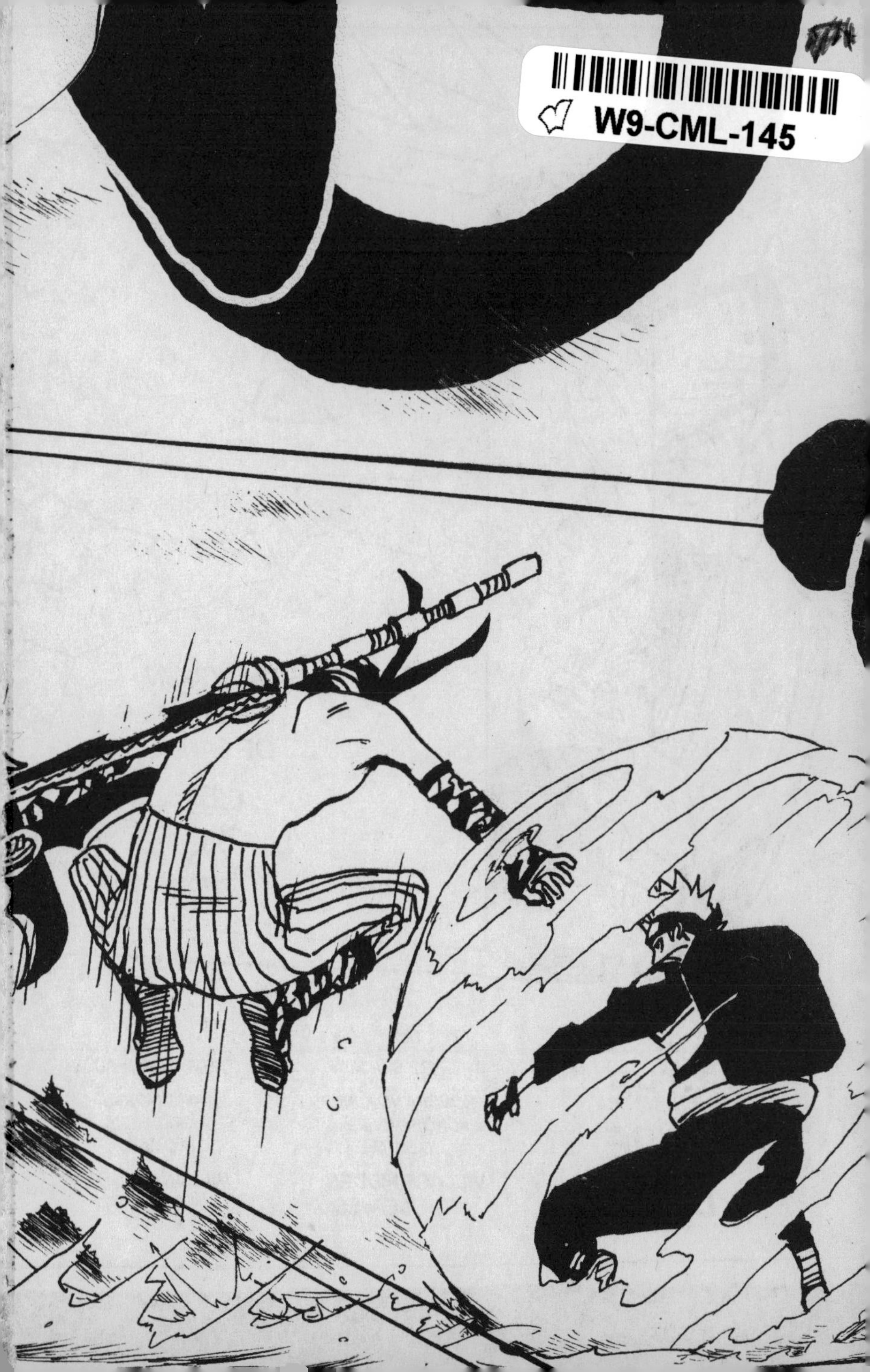

**IWA NO KUNI:
THE LAND
OF STONES**

**SUNA NO KUNI:
THE LAND
OF SAND**

**THE
FIVE
LANDS**

THE FIRE SHADOW

*KONOHA NO KUNI
KONOHARGURE
NO SATO:*

**VILLAGE HIDDEN
IN THE LEAVES**

THE WATER SHADOW

*KIRO NO KUNI
KIRIGAKURE
NO SATO:*

**VILLAGE HIDDEN
IN THE MIST**

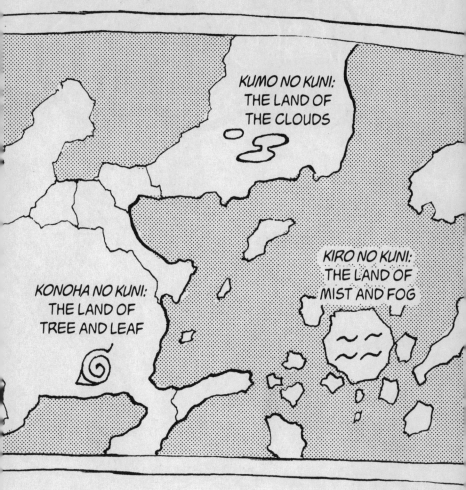

KUMO NO KUNI:
THE LAND OF
THE CLOUDS

KIRO NO KUNI:
THE LAND OF
MIST AND FOG

KONOHA NO KUNI:
THE LAND OF
TREE AND LEAF

THE LIGHTNING SHADOW

KUMO NO KUNI
KUMOGAKURE
NO SATO:

**VILLAGE HIDDEN
IN THE CLOUDS**

THE WIND SHADOW

SUNA NO KUNI
SUNAGAKURE
NO SATO:

**VILLAGE HIDDEN
IN THE SAND**

THE EARTH SHADOW

IWA NO KUNI
IWAGAKURE
NO SATO:

**VILLAGE HIDDEN
IN THE SHADOW**

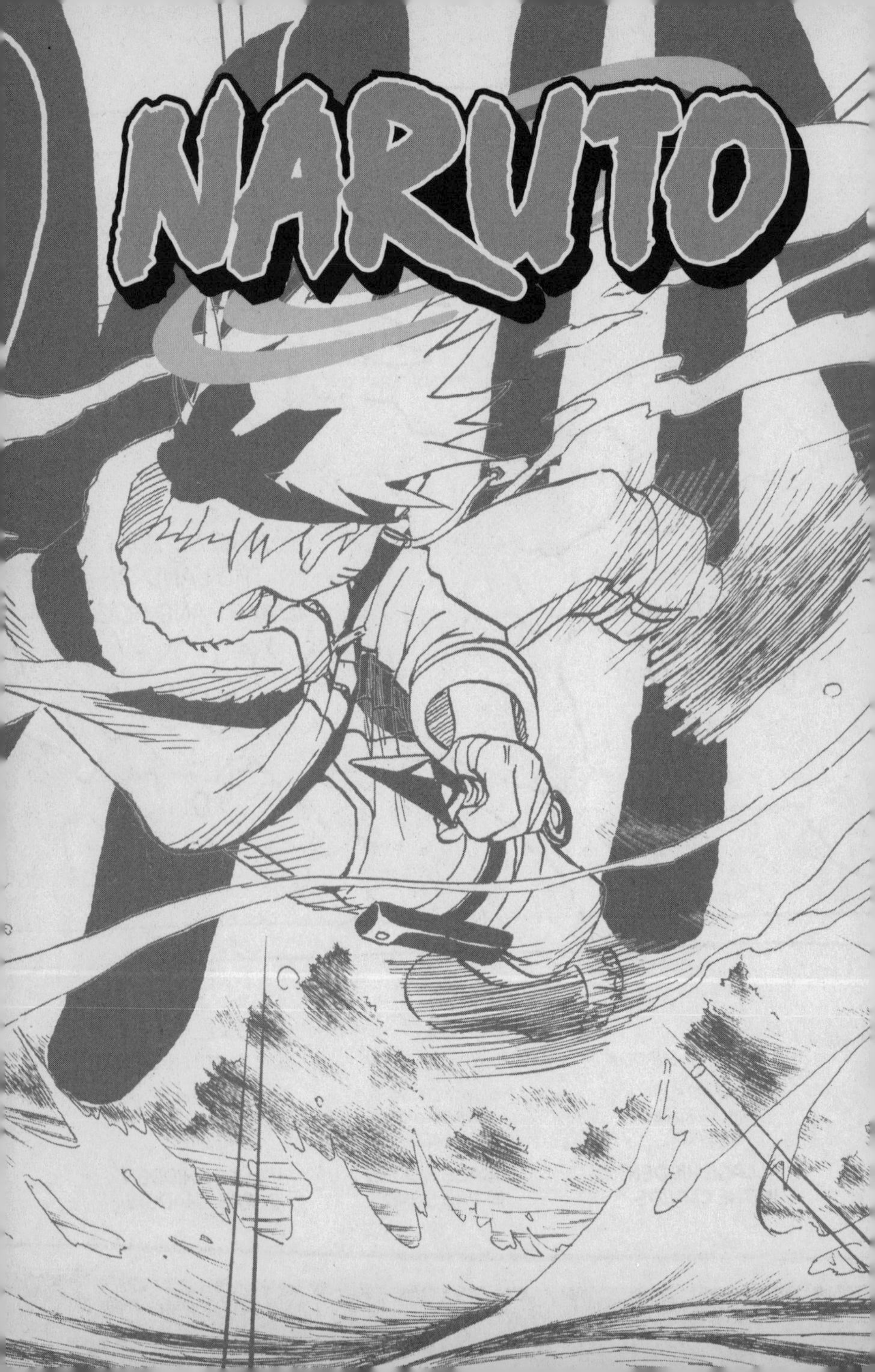
NARUTO

THE SECRET PLAN

ORIGINAL STORY BY **MASASHI KISHIMOTO**
ADAPTED BY TRACEY WEST

vizkids

VIZ MEDIA
SAN FRANCISCO

NARUTO THE SECRET PLAN
CHAPTER BOOK 4

Illustrations: Masashi Kishimoto
Design: Courtney Utt

NARUTO © 1999 by Masashi Kishimoto. All rights reserved.
Original manga first published in Japan in 1999 by SHUEISHA Inc., Tokyo. This
English language chapter book novelization is based on the original manga. The
stories, characters and incidents mentioned in this publication are entirely fictional.

Published by VIZ Media, LLC
P.O. Box 77010
San Francisco, CA 94107

www.viz.com

West, Tracey, 1965-
 The secret plan / original story by Masashi Kishimoto ; adapted by
Tracey West ; [illustrations, Masashi Kishimoto].
   p. cm. -- (Naruto ; 4)
 Summary: During their first assignment to protect a famous bridge builder, Naruto and two
other junior ninjas face a formidable opponent in Zabuza, the evil Demon of the Mist.
 ISBN-13: 978-1-4215-2314-9
 ISBN-10: 1-4215-2314-0
 [1. Ninja--Fiction. 2. Japan--Fiction.] I. Kishimoto, Masashi, 1974- II. Title. PZ7.W51937Sd 2008
 [Fic]--dc22
            2008020231

Printed in the U.S.A.
First printing, November 2008

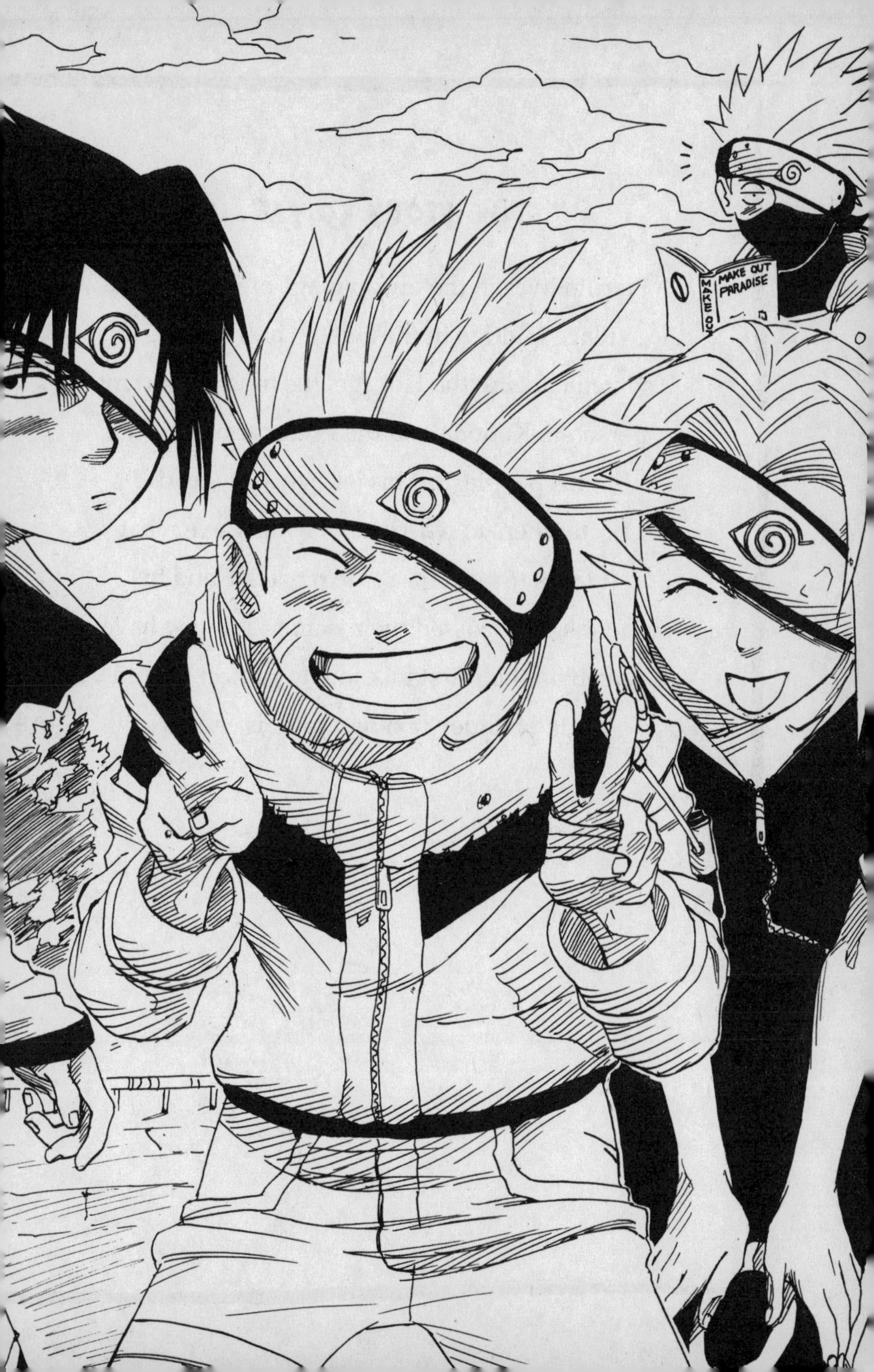
MAKE OUT PARADISE
MAKE OUT

THE STORY SO FAR...

Naruto lives in the ninja village of Konoha, the Village Hidden in the Leaves, and dreams of someday being the Hokage, the most important person in Konoha and the leader and protector of his people. But his jokester ways cause his teachers to worry he may not have what it takes to become a true ninja. He and his friends have passed their exams and now have taken on their first mission, to protect the old bridge builder Tazuna from his enemies.

Naruto
ナルト

Naruto is training to be a ninja. He's a bit of a clown. But deep down, he's serious about becoming the world's greatest shinobi!

Sakura
春野サクラ

Naruto and Sasuke's classmate. She has a crush on Sasuke, who ignores her. In return, she picks on Naruto, who has a crush on *her*.

Sasuke
うちはサスケ

The top student in Naruto's class and a member of the prestigious Uchiha clan.

NARUTO UZUMAKI stared up at the tall tree. He was short for his age, but his spiked blond hair added a few inches to his height. The blue headband he wore had a metal plate attached to it that was carved with the symbol of the Leaf Village. Only ninja could wear the headband, and Naruto wore it with pride.

Naruto had never seen a sword as big as the one stuck into the tree trunk. A fierce-looking ninja balanced on the blade of the sword.

Just days earlier Naruto had been back in the Leaf Village, starting his training as a genin, a junior ninja. He was part of Squad Seven along with two other genin, Sakura and Sasuke. Lord Hokage, the village leader, had given them easy tasks, like babysitting and helping farmers. But Naruto had complained. He wanted more action.

Lord Hokage gave in. He asked Squad Seven to escort an old bridge builder, Tazuna, to his home in the Land of Waves. Squad Seven's sensei, Kakashi, led the way as their teacher.

It should have been a simple mission. But an evil man named Gato wanted the bridge builder gone. He hired ninja to do his dirty work for him. First the terrible Oni Brothers attacked. They'd left Naruto with a wound in his hand before Kakashi defeated them. But the Oni Brothers were just the beginning of their troubles.

This ninja in the tree wore striped trousers tucked into camouflage boots. Matching armbands covered his bare arms from wrist to armpit. A mask hid the lower half of his face. His headband was wrapped diagonally around his spiky black hair. He had no eyebrows, giving him a strange, sinister look.

The sudden appearance of the ninja startled the students. But Kakashi, their sensei, was calm, as always. He stepped forward. Squad Seven and Tazuna, the old bridge builder, stood behind him. Naruto clenched his fists, ready to fight. Next to him was

Sakura, a pretty girl with pale pink hair. Then came Sasuke, a boy whose dark, serious eyes were fixed on the ninja in the tree.

"Well, if it isn't Zabuza, the kid who ran off and left the Land of Mist," Kakashi said.

Zabuza glared down at him from his perch. "You are Kakashi of the Sharingan Eye, I presume? Hand over the old man!"

Sharingan eye? Naruto wondered. *What the heck does that mean?*

"Assume the battle formation," Kakashi told his squad. "Protect Mr. Tazuna. This situation demands teamwork. All of you stay out of the fight."

Kakashi reached for his leaf headband. He always wore his headband down over his left eye. Now he pushed it up and opened his eye.

"Oh man!" Naruto gasped. The center of Kakashi's eye was bright red. Black, teardrop-shaped symbols swirled around his pupil.

What's up with his eye? Naruto wondered.

"This is an honor," Zabuza said. "To face the legendary Mirror Wheel Eye so soon after we meet."

"What is it?" Naruto asked. "A mirror wheel eye? A sharingan eye?"

"Ninja who have the Sharingan Eye have mastered a form of ninjutsu," Sasuke explained. "It allows them to see the reality behind any illusion or spell. It also allows them to reflect the power of an attack back on an attacker. Only the most skilled ninja can master the Sharingan Eye. And there's more."

"Like what?" Naruto asked.

Above them, Zabuza laughed. "Oh yes, there's more. The most impressive ability of the Sharingan Eye is that it allows its master to learn and copy his opponent's attack," he said, looking at Kakashi. "When I worked for the Village in the Mist, I owned the usual bingo book—the *Who's Who* of our enemies. It had a long write-up on you, the man who copied one thousand ninjutsu—Kakashi, the Mirror Ninja."

Kakashi's the best! Naruto thought with pride.

Our teacher, a legendary ninja? Sakura wondered.

Sasuke was thinking too. *The Sharingan Eye is supposed to be unique to the Uchiha clan—my clan. Could he be...?*

"The time for talk is over," Zabuza announced. "I'm on a very tight schedule to finish off the old man."

Squad Seven suddenly remembered the order from Kakashi. They quickly flew into defensive formation around the bridge builder, Tazuna. They each held a throwing knife—a kunai—ready to protect the man from Zabuza.

"I see, Kakashi," Zabuza said. "It looks like I'm going to have to take you out first."

The ninja jumped off his sword, moving so quickly that Naruto couldn't see him. He took the sword with him. Suddenly, there was a splash from a lake at the edge of the woods.

"Over there!" Naruto yelled.

Zabuza rose up out of the lake and stood on top of the water. Water swirled around him. His left arm was raised in the air, and he held his right hand in front of his face, palm sideways, two of his fingers against his mouth.

"Is he walking on water?" Sakura asked.

He's clever, Kakashi thought. *He's built up a great deal of chakra. The finest of the ninja arts… the Kirigakure jutsu.*

The water whirled up around Zabuza, surrounding him. When the waves splashed down, Zabuza was gone.

"He will come after me first," Kakashi said. "Zabuza is a master of the art of stealth. If you let your guard down for a moment, he will destroy you. I haven't mastered every aspect of the Sharingan Eye yet. So all of you stay on your toes!"

Naruto, Sakura, and Sasuke got ready to battle. They scanned the trees for any sign of the enemy ninja. But a white fog rose up from the lake, making it difficult to see.

"What's with all the fog?" Naruto complained.

Zabuza could attack them at any moment—and they couldn't even see him coming!

2

KAKASHI QUICKLY formed a hand sign with the fingers of his right hand. Naruto knew that hand signs were used in the most difficult ninja moves. The sensei's body was completely still as he waited for Zabuza to strike.

An eerie quiet came over them all. Zabuza was out there, somewhere, in the fog. But they couldn't see him coming.

The suspense was too much for Sasuke.

If he even sees me blink, he'll destroy me. I can

feel it, he thought. Beads of cold sweat poured down his face. *I can't stay like this for long. I'm going to lose it. Knowing my life is in the hands of a master ninja…I hate it!*

Kakashi sensed Sasuke's feelings.

"Sasuke, calm down," the sensei said sternly. "Even if he gets me, I'll still protect you. I will **NEVER** let my comrades down."

"I wouldn't bet on it!"

Zabuza's voice cut through the mist. Then he appeared out of nowhere. The ninja had landed right in front of Tazuna!

"*Game over,*" Zabuza said.

Kakashi swiftly turned and focused the Sharingan Eye on Zabuza. Then he moved fast, sprinting across the grass in a blur. In the next moment, Kakashi slammed into

Zabuza's body. Squad Seven and Tazuna tumbled backward.

A trickle of water flowed from Zabuza's hurt body. The water dripped down onto the grass.

Then Naruto saw something behind Kakashi—another Zabuza! This Zabuza had his sword drawn, ready to strike.

"**MASTER,** behind you!" Naruto yelled.

As Kakashi turned, the first Zabuza dissolved into water and splashed to the ground. The second Zabuza rushed at Kakashi with his sword.

Naruto gasped. Then Kakashi's body turned into water too!

Zabuza knew what had happened. He had created a water doppelganger—a double of

himself made out of water—to fool Kakashi.
But Kakashi had copied the attack. He had
created a water doppelganger of himself.

He was able to copy me in this mist? Zabuza
thought.

"Don't move," said a voice behind Zabuza.
It was Kakashi.

"*Game over,*" Kakashi said.

"Awesome!" Naruto cheered. Sakura was so relieved that she laughed.

Zabuza laughed too—a low, sinister laugh.

"You think it's over? You just don't get it," the ninja said. "It will take more to defeat me than copying me like an ape. But you are good. You gave that speech to your squad to distract me. Then you copied my water clone jutsu. Too bad for you...I'm not that easy to fool!"

A *third* Zabuza appeared behind Kakashi. The sensei struck out at the Zabuza in front of him, but the ninja turned into liquid and splashed to the ground.

"The second Zabuza was a water doppelganger too!" Naruto cried out.

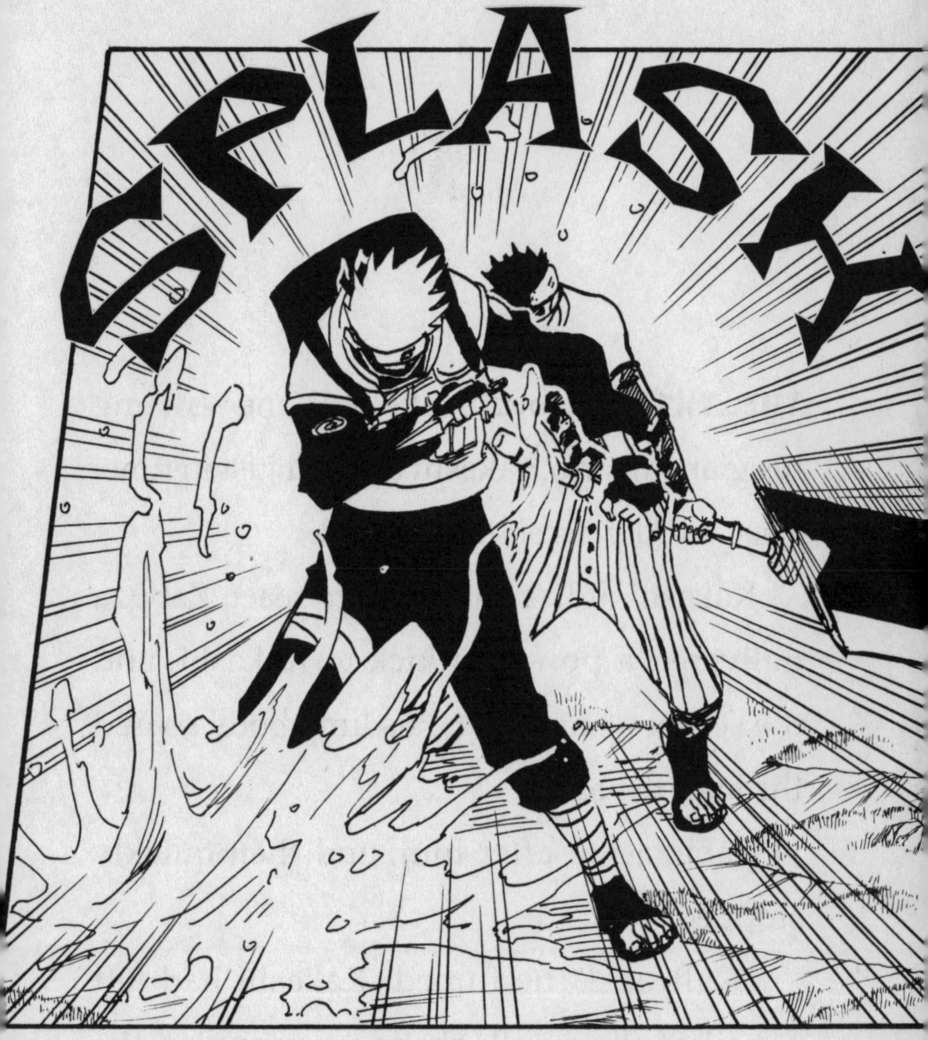
SPLASH

THE THIRD Zabuza—the real one—swung his giant sword. Kakashi ducked just in time. The sword pierced the ground.

Kakashi didn't have time to react. Zabuza delivered a powerful kick to Kakashi, and the sensei went flying. His limp body soared through the air.

Zabuza ran after him, and then quickly stopped.

"Caltrops!" he fumed. Kakashi had left a trail of the small, sharp weapons on the ground to slow down Zabuza.

Kakashi landed in the lake with a splash.

"Master!" Naruto yelled.

Sakura's green eyes were wide with disbelief. *Did Master Kakashi get kicked all that way?*

Zabuza's techniques are amazing! Sasuke thought.

In the lake, Kakashi struggled to stay above water.

It's so heavy…but why?

Zabuza stood on the shore. His dark eyes glittered as he began to perform a series of hand signs.

"Ha! You fool!" he said. "Art of the Water Prison!"

Kakashi's body tensed. *I landed in the*

water so I could regroup, but I guess that was a mistake. It was too late to fight Zabuza's attack now.

A loud **GONG!** filled the air as the Water Prison jutsu began to form. Zabuza thrust his hand into the heavy water. The water formed a huge bubble around Kakashi, trapping him inside. The bubble rose above the lake.

"You can't escape this prison!" Zabuza cried. "You're trapped!"

Kakashi stood in the bubble, helpless, as Zabuza taunted him.

"Your running around free makes it hard for me to do my job," Zabuza said. "I'll finish you later...after I've taken care of the others."

He performed a hand sign with his free

hand. "Art of the Water Doppelganger!"

As he spoke, another clone of Zabuza formed in the lake water.

I knew he was good, but not this good, Kakashi thought.

The clone walked onto land and looked right at Naruto. The clone didn't speak. Instead, Zabuza did all the talking as he kept Kakashi prisoner in the lake.

"Little ninja wannabes," Zabuza said. "You even wear ninja headbands, trying to fit in. But a true ninja is one who has crossed the barrier between the living and the dead. Clothes don't make you a ninja. You need skills good enough to put you in my bingo book of enemies before you deserve to be called a ninja."

The doppelganger made a hand sign. A mist began to form around him.

"We don't call your kind 'ninja,'" Zabuza said. "We call them…"

The Zabuza clone disappeared before he finished his sentence.

"He vanished again!" Naruto yelled.

Then the clone appeared out of nowhere and kicked Naruto in the chest. Naruto fell back—and his headband flew off. It landed in front of the clone. The Zabuza clone stomped on the headband with his right foot.

"…brats!" Zabuza finished.

"Everyone, listen!" Kakashi called out. "Take Tazuna and go! It's a fight you can't win. If Zabuza wants to hold me in this water prison, he can't leave this place. So get out of here!"

Naruto's first instinct was to obey his sensei. He pushed down on the ground, trying to get back on his feet. The wound in his left hand throbbed.

The pain triggered something in Naruto. He remembered the promise he had made to himself when the Oni Brothers hurt his hand.

I swear, by the pain in my left hand, that I will protect the old man until this mission is done. I won't freeze up. I won't get scared.

Sasuke had jumped in to save him then. After that, Naruto had vowed never to back down again.

He *couldn't* back down. He had trained hard—and fought hard—to earn his leaf headband. He was a ninja now.

Naruto stood up and glared at the Zabuza doppelganger.

"I said I'd **NEVER** run away again," Naruto said. "And I'm not running away now!"

With an angry growl, he charged at Zabuza.

4

"STOP, YOU FOOL!" Kakashi yelled.

"Naruto, what are you doing?" Sakura called out.

Naruto ignored them both. He reached the clone, who punched back at Naruto with a powerful arm. Naruto skidded back across the ground.

Sakura ran to him. "What were you thinking, tackling him by yourself? You're a junior ninja! You can't—"

Sakura stopped. Naruto was breathing

hard. He held something in his hand and slowly raised his arm to show them.

"It's his leaf headband," Sakura realized. Naruto had grabbed it back when he attacked the clone.

"Hey, you!" Naruto called out. He was bent over, still in pain from the clone's punch. "What's life like without eyebrows, you freak? I've got a new listing for your bingo book right here. A ninja who is going to be the next Lord Hokage of the Leaf Village."

Naruto stood up straight and glared at the clone. **"NARUTO UZUMAKI!"**

Tazuna was impressed. *When we first met, I thought that little fellow was just a brat. But look at him now!*

"Sasuke, listen up," Naruto said, keeping

his eyes on the clone. "There's something I want to tell you."

"What is it?" Sasuke asked.

"I have a plan," Naruto replied.

Great, now *he has a plan?* Sasuke thought. But what he said was, "So it's time for some teamwork?"

New feelings were rising in Sakura. *I feel strange. Naruto is so...*

"Okay! **Let's get busy!**" Naruto said. His blue eyes flashed with inner fire. "Time for us to rock and roll!"

"Heh heh," Zabuza laughed. "You're very sure of yourself. But do you really think you stand a chance against me?"

"What's the matter with you?" Kakashi yelled from inside the bubble. "I told you to run. It's over. It was over the second he caught me. You have to do your duty. We're here to protect Mr. Tazuna!"

Naruto turned to the bridge builder. "Gramps?"

Tazuna sighed. "Let's face it, I got us into this mess by lying. I've had a real long life, and it would be wrong to let you kids get hurt trying to save me. I have nothing to lose."

He looked Naruto in the eye. "You go ahead. Give this fight everything you've got."

Sasuke clenched his fists. "So that's it!"

"Are you ready for this?" Naruto asked Zabuza.

The clone laughed. "You're playing at being a ninja like it's a child's game. But when

I was your age, I had already destroyed more ninja than you can count."

Naruto gasped. *Could it really be true?*

"The Demon Zabuza," Kakashi said from inside his water prison. "In the Village Hidden in the Mist, the final step toward becoming a ninja is extremely difficult."

"So you've heard of our little graduation test?" Zabuza asked. "It's the ultimate battle between classmates."

Kakashi explained. "Students who had been friends were divided into pairs. They were forced to fight against each other—a long, brutal fight to the end. Ten years ago, the elders of the village had to reform the test, all because of one human fiend."

"What kind of reform?" Sakura asked.

"What fiend are you talking about?"

"It was a boy who hadn't even qualified as a ninja," Kakashi went on. "He cruelly attacked *one hundred* members of his class."

Zabuza grinned. "Ahh, yes. Good times," he said, his voice eerily happy. "I used to have such fun."

The story filled the junior ninja with horror. Then, without warning, the Zabuza doppelganger charged at Sasuke. He reached out with a powerful arm and caught Sasuke around the neck. Then he slammed Sasuke into the ground and stepped on his chest.

"Sasuke!" Sakura screamed.

Naruto made a hand signal in front of his face. "Art of the Doppelganger!"

A loud **SHOOOM!** filled the air, and in

the next instant, an army of Naruto clones appeared out of nowhere. They formed a wide circle around the Zabuza clone.

"So, doppelgangers, eh?" the Zabuza clone said. He stepped off of Sasuke. "And quite a lot of them."

Each Naruto clone whipped out a sharp kunai. Their eyes gleamed, eager to battle.

"Ready or not!" the Naruto clones yelled.

They surged toward the Zabuza clone all at once. For a second, it looked like they had taken him down. Then...

WHAM! The Zabuza clone struck out in every direction, sending all of the Narutos flying backward. The Naruto clones disappeared as they hit the ground one by one.

One Naruto skidded to a stop in the dirt.

He reached inside a pocket in his orange pants. *This is the last thing that might work...*

"Sasuke!" Naruto yelled out. He threw an object at Sasuke—a windmill shuriken, a large throwing star with folding blades.

Sasuke caught the shuriken. *So that's what Naruto's got in mind. Excellent. Much better than I expected.* He whirled around. Then he unfurled the weapon to release all four large, curved blades. He held the shuriken in front of his face.

"Demon Wind Shuriken! **WINDMILL OF SHADOWS!**" he yelled. He jumped up in the air and hurled the weapon at the Zabuza clone.

"Shuriken are useless against me," the clone said, grabbing his sword.

But the shuriken flew right past the clone—just as Sasuke wanted. Instead, it zoomed right toward the real Zabuza in the lake.

"At least this time you had the sense to attack my true form," Zabuza said calmly. He reached out with his free hand and expertly caught the shuriken.

"Amateur," he scoffed.

Then another shuriken appeared right behind it! Zabuza was surprised. "A second shuriken in the shadow of the first shuriken!"

Kakashi watched the attack from inside his water prison. *He used the art of the shadow shuriken,* the sensei realized.

The shadow shuriken was aimed right at

Zabuza's chest. He couldn't catch it without letting go of Kakashi's water prison. Instead, the ninja jumped up in the air. The shuriken flew right underneath him.

"Still an amateur," Zabuza taunted.

"He dodged it!" Sakura cried in disbelief.

But Sasuke gave a small laugh. His attack was far from over…

BONG!

The shadow shuriken transformed in midair—into Naruto!

"Here goes nothing!" Naruto shouted. He threw a kunai at Zabuza's right hand. The ninja turned and saw it coming—there was nothing he could do. He pulled his hand out of the water prison to dodge the knife.

Naruto splashed down into the water.

Zabuza turned to him, his eyes blood red with rage. Back on land, Sasuke, Sakura, and Tazuna watched in disbelief. Naruto was helpless now. He could barely swim. How could he defend himself against a ninja who could walk on water?

"That little runt!" Zabuza charged across the top of the water, bringing the blade of the windmill shuriken down, aiming for Naruto.

CLANG!

Kakashi's hand rose up from the water. The metal plate on the back of his glove stopped the blade as it came down. Zabuza gasped.

"Master Kakashi!" Sakura yelled.

5

WATER DRIPPED down Kakashi's face. He kept a tight grip on the shuriken.

"Naruto, your scheme was brilliant," he called out. "You've learned so much, all of you."

Naruto laughed. "My shadow clone jutsu wasn't meant to take down Zabuza at all. It kept his attention away from me while I transformed myself into the second wind shuriken. One of my clones threw it to Sasuke. He stacked it on top of a shuriken he already had and threw them both at Zabuza. Of course, I didn't think I'd be able to defeat him that way, but at least I was able to free you from the water prison."

Zabuza weakly lifted his head, still caught in Kakashi's grasp. "So, you made me fly into such a rage that I broke the spell holding the water prison together."

"No, you didn't break your own spell," Kakashi told him. "It was broken from without, when Naruto threw his kunai at you."

Zabuza gave an annoyed grunt.

"Just so you know, the same spell won't work on me twice," Kakashi said. "Your move."

Zabuza pulled away from Kakashi and stepped across the water. The two ninja faced each other. Kakashi fixed his Sharingan Eye on Zabuza.

Zabuza made a series of hand signals, one after the other. He chanted their names under his breath.

Using his Sharingan Eye, Kakashi made the same moves, exactly as Zabuza made them.

"Water Style! Water Dragon Missile!" both ninja shouted at the same time.

BOOM! A huge wave of water rose up in front of each ninja. Each giant wave took the shape of a long-necked dragon. The two waves slammed into each other. Then the water crashed back onto the top of the lake. Naruto held his breath as the water covered him. The wave drenched Sasuke, Sakura, and

Tazuna as they stood on the shore.

So many hand signals! And Master Kakashi copied them all perfectly, Sasuke realized.

Sakura protected Tazuna from the crashing waves. The battle between the elite ninja astonished her. *What are they doing? Is it ninjutsu?* In a ninjutsu attack, a ninja performed superhuman feats.

Zabuza ran across the water and swung his sword over his head. Kakashi grabbed it between his hands. The two ninja stared at each other, both refusing to back down.

Something isn't right, Zabuza thought. He quickly jumped back. Kakashi jumped back at exactly the same time.

Zabuza dashed to the right. Kakashi moved right at the same moment.

Zabuza stopped, then dashed to the left. Kakashi did the same.

Then Zabuza raised his left hand above his head. He made a hand sign with his right hand, holding his first two fingers in front of his mouth.

Kakashi made the exact same moves!

Zabuza's mind raced. *It's impossible. He sees...*

"Through all your attacks?" Kakashi said out loud.

Zabuza gasped. *He's reading my mind! Curse him. He's...*

"Got that evil look in his eye, right?" Kakashi finished for him.

Zabuza was losing confidence. "You're just a poor copy of me! I'm the real thing.

No copycat stands a chance against me!" His voice grew louder. "You mimic me like a parrot! I'll close your beak for good!"

Then Zabuza's eyes widened. A figure was appearing behind Kakashi. It was a clone—a clone of Zabuza!

Me? But that's impossible! It has to be one of his illusions, Zabuza guessed.

Kakashi quickly performed several hand signals. "Water style! **GIANT WATERFALL!**" he cried out. His Sharingan Eye glowed with red fire.

"What?!" Zabuza yelled. It couldn't be. Kakashi had used his own attack against him—before he had even finished it!

A gigantic wave surged up from the lake, towering above the surrounding trees. The wave picked up Zabuza and carried him to the shore. He landed against a tree. Kakashi jumped onto a branch above him. Zabuza looked up at his enemy.

"Why? Can you predict the future?" Zabuza asked wearily.

"I predict...your *end,*" Kakashi informed him.

Kakashi crouched down, ready to attack. Sunlight glinted off his kunai.

Suddenly, two silver throwing needles flew through the air before Kakashi could attack. The needles struck Zabuza, and the ninja collapsed to the ground.

On a nearby tree branch, a mysterious ninja watched the needles hit Zabuza. The ninja wore a short robe and sash over striped pants and a shirt. A mask with a strange, swirled symbol hid the ninja's entire face.

The ninja nodded.

"Ha. Your prediction came true!"

6

NARUTO SPLASHED out of the lake and ran toward the trees. Kakashi jumped down from the tree branch.

The ninja in the tree bowed. "Thank you for your help," said a soft voice. "I hope you don't mind my interfering. But I wanted the satisfaction of taking care of Zabuza myself."

"The mask is familiar," Kakashi said. "Correct me if I'm wrong. Aren't you a ninja hunter from the Mist Village?"

"Well, aren't you a smart one?" the ninja replied.

"A 'ninja hunter'?" Sakura asked.

"I am, indeed, a member of the elite tracking unit from the Mist Village. It is our duty—and our art—to deal with rogue ninja and outlaws," the ninja explained.

Kakashi eyed the ninja carefully. The strange ninja was short and slim. The ninja's hair was long in back, and two tails hung down the front. *This ninja looks and sounds like a kid*, Kakashi realized. *Not much older than Naruto or my other students. Such a young ninja hunter! This isn't your average kid, that's for sure.*

Naruto skidded to a stop in front of the ninja's tree. He looked over at Zabuza's fallen body. Then he looked up at the ninja hunter.

"What's going on here?" he asked angrily.
"WHO ARE YOU?"

"Relax, Naruto. This isn't an enemy," Kakashi told him.

"That's not what I asked! What I mean

is—this hunter or whatever brought down Zabuza, who wasn't exactly a pushover!" Naruto fumed. "Zabuza got taken out by a kid who's about my age like it was nothing! What, do we stink or something? What's up with that?"

Kakashi stood up. "Oh," he said, finally understanding. "I can see how a thing like that would be hard to accept. But it's a fact you'll have to live with."

Naruto grimaced as Kakashi patted him on the head.

"This probably won't be the last time we run into someone who's both younger than you...and stronger than *me*," the sensei informed him.

Naruto looked away. He was still angry.

Sasuke grunted. He didn't like that idea much either.

The ninja hunter jumped down from the tree in one quick, graceful movement, then knelt next to Zabuza's body.

"Your battle is over. I must get rid of the evidence, to protect its secrets from our enemies," the ninja said. The kid hoisted Zabuza up. "I'm off."

A light wind whipped up around the ninja. The wind died an instant later—and the ninja hunter had vanished.

"The kid's gone!" Naruto cried.

KAKASHI PULLED his headband down over his Sharingan Eye.

"Now we still have to escort Mr. Tazuna the rest of the way to his home," he told his students. "Let's put our best feet forward."

Tazuna laughed. "Ha! You kids must be so humiliated! But never mind. Sorry about all the trouble. You can rest up at my house."

Naruto was about to give Tazuna a piece of his mind when he saw Kakashi sway on his feet. The ninja fell forward, landing face down in the dirt.

"Master Kakashi!" Naruto yelled.

"I must have used the Sharingan Eye too much," Kakashi said weakly. "Can't move."

Kakashi closed his eyes. When he opened them again, he found himself on a mattress in a bright, clean room. His students sat on the floor around him, along with Tazuna. They must have safely reached Tazuna's house, he thought. A dark-haired woman stood over him. She was Tazuna's daughter, Tsunami.

"Are you all right, teacher?" she asked with her hands on her hips.

"No, but I will be in about a week," Kakashi replied.

"The Sharingan Eye is an incredible power," Sakura said. "But it puts such a strain on your body. Is it worth it?"

Tazuna answered for him. "Ha! This time you took down our biggest enemy yet. So we can probably relax for a while."

Sakura cupped her chin with her hand. "I still can't get my mind off that masked kid."

"That mask is worn by the most elite and secret ninja in the Mist Village," Kakashi told her. "The ninja hunters all wear them. Their job is to make sure a ninja is really dead. Then they report back to their village."

Back in the woods, the mysterious ninja knelt over Zabuza's body. The ninja unwrapped a cloth containing several knives of different shapes and sizes. Then the ninja hunter moved to cut away the mask around Zabuza's mouth.

Suddenly, Zabuza grabbed the ninja's hand. **"ENOUGH!"** Zabuza cried, sitting up. "I can do it myself!"

"Well, well," the ninja hunter said. "Awake already?"

Zabuza sat up. He yanked at the throwing needles lodged in his neck. "You're about as skilled as a butcher," he complained.

"Gently please, Zabuza, sir, or you'll really hurt yourself," the ninja hunter warned.

Zabuza ignored the ninja and pulled out the needles, throwing them on the grass. "How long are you going to keep that mask on? Take it off!" he demanded.

"Old habits die hard." The ninja took off the mask and revealed a pretty, young face.

"They would have killed you if I hadn't intervened," the ninja said.

"But you didn't have to hit my neck to put me in that deathlike trance," Zabuza pointed

out. "You're such a brutal little brat!"

"Exactly," the ninja replied with a grin. "Besides, the neck is less muscular than other points in the body. It was easier for me to target the pressure points. That would leave an ordinary target unable to move for about a week. But of course, someone like you will recover more quickly, right?"

Zabuza shook his head. "You're so innocent and so smart at the same time. I guess that's why I like you."

"Well, I am still a *kid*," the ninja said, standing up. "The mist has lifted. Next time... will you be all right?"

Zabuza's eyes became dark with anger. **"NEXT TIME...I'LL BREAK THE SHARINGAN SPELL!"** he promised.

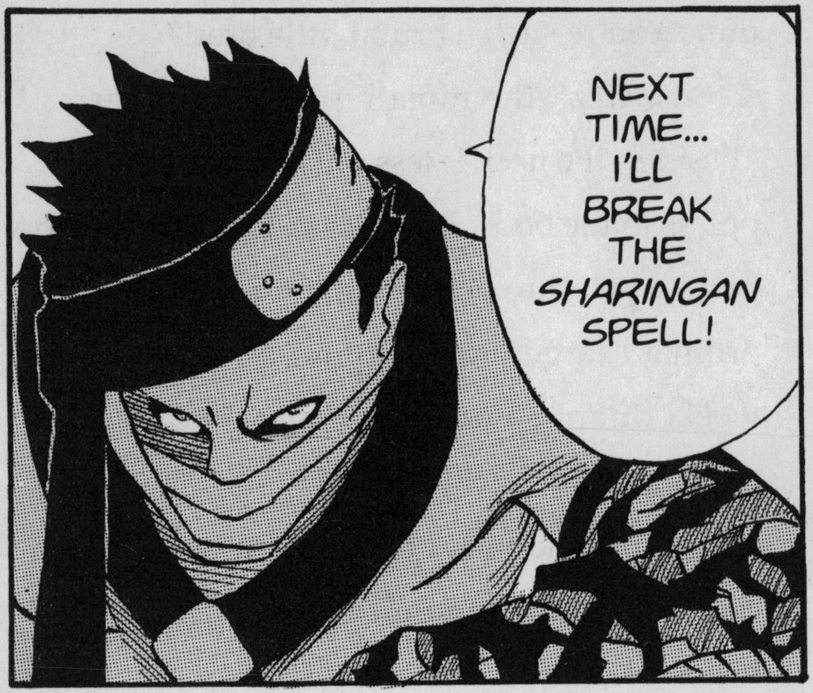
NEXT TIME... I'LL BREAK THE SHARINGAN SPELL!

KAKASHI OPENED his eye, drawn out of a deep sleep by a sudden feeling of panic. Naruto and Sakura were standing over him. They screamed and jumped back, startled. Naruto fell flat on his back.

"Don't be such a klutz!" Sakura scolded. "We almost got to see what was behind his mask!"

But Kakashi wasn't worried about his curious students. "It's odd," he said. "I know Zabuza is dead. But I still can't shake a strong feeling that there's something I missed. Something big!"

Kakashi sat up and held his chin in his right hand, thinking.

"What's wrong, Master Kakashi?" Naruto asked.

"The ninja hunter took Zabuza away," Kakashi pointed out. "But why? There was no reason to. And there's also a mystery around the weapons the ninja hunter used—acupuncture needles."

Sasuke raised an eyebrow. "No way!"

"Yes way!" Kakashi said.

"What nonsense are you talking about?" Tazuna asked, scratching his head.

"That it's likely **Zabuza is still alive!**" Kakashi announced.

Naruto, Sakura, and Tazuna all gaped in astonishment.

Zabuza, alive?

How?

They had all seen him fall.

If he had not really died…If it was a trick… If he was alive, then their true battle was far from over.

Zabuza could return at any moment. They would have to be ready!

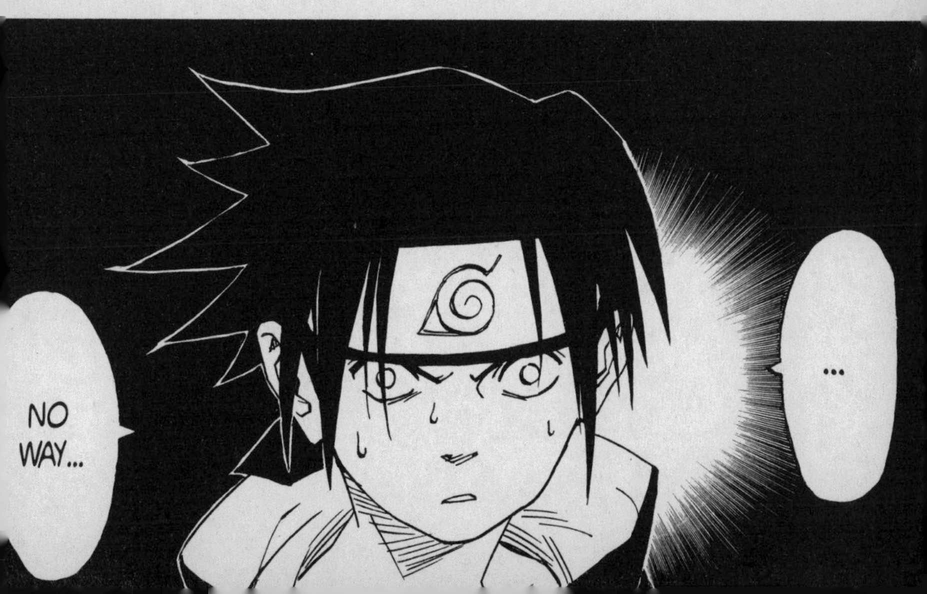
...
NO WAY...

Ninja Terms

Hokage

The leader and protector of the Village Hidden in the Leaves. Only the strongest and wisest ninja can achieve this rank.

Jutsu

Jutsu means "arts" or "techniques." Sometimes referred to as *ninjutsu*, which means more specifically the jutsu of a ninja.

Bunshin

Translated as "doppelganger," this is the art of creating multiple versions of yourself.

Sensei

Teacher

Shuriken

A ninja weapon, a throwing star

About the Authors

Author/artist **Masashi Kishimoto** was born in 1974 in rural Okayama Prefecture, Japan. After spending time in art college, he won the Hop Step Award for new manga artists with his manga *Karakuri* (Mechanism). Kishimoto decided to base his next story on traditional Japanese culture. His first version of *Naruto*, drawn in 1997, was a one-shot story about fox spirits; his final version, which debuted in *Weekly Shonen Jump* in 1999, quickly became the most popular ninja manga in Japan. This book is based on that manga.

......

Tracey West is the author of more than 150 books for children and young adults, including the *Pixie Tricks* and *Scream Shop* series. An avid fan of cartoons, comic books, and manga, she has appeared on the New York Times Best Seller List as the author of the Pokémon chapter book adaptations. She currently lives with her family in New York State's Hudson Valley.

The Story of Naruto continues in:
Chapter Book 5
Bridge of Courage

Naruto and his ninja friends Sasuke and Sakura

are working hard trying to keep crabby old

bridge-builder Tazuna safe from his enemies

while he finishes his new project. But while

Naruto and his friends continue to train and

learn more about Tazuna's family and past,

their enemy Zabuza plans his return attack!

COLLECT THEM ALL!

#1 THE BOY NINJA

#2 THE TESTS OF A NINJA

#3 THE WORST JOB

#4 THE SECRET PLAN

COMING SOON!

#5 BRIDGE OF COURAGE

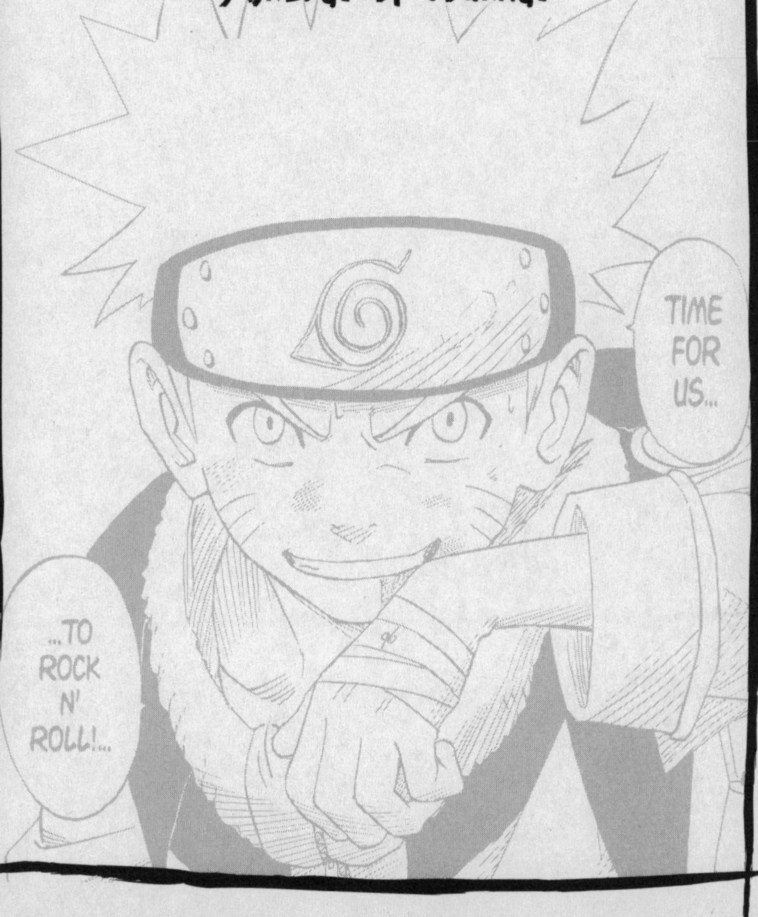
TIME FOR US...
...TO ROCK N' ROLL!...